IT'S MINE!

LET'S TRY TO SHARE

By Janine Amos and Annabel Spenceley
Consultant Rachael Underwood

Published in the United States by Windmill Books (Alphabet Soup)
Windmill Books
303 Park Avenue South
Suite #1280
New York, NY 10010-3657

Library of Congress Cataloging-in-Publication Data

Amos, Janine
      It's mine! : let's try to share / by Janine Amos and Annabel Spenceley.
           p. cm. – (Best behavior)
      Contents: The treasure map—The tiger mask.
      Summary: Two brief stories demonstrate the importance of sharing.
      ISBN 978-1-60754-028-1 (lib.)—978-1-60754-048-9 (pbk.)
978-1-60754-049-6 (6 pack)
      1. Social interaction in children—Juvenile literature   2. Problem solving in
children—Juvenile literature   [1. Sharing   2. Behavior   3. Etiquette   4. Conduct of
life]   Spenceley, Annabel   II. Title   III. Series
      177'.1—dc22

American Library Binding 13-digit ISBN: 978-1-60754-028-1
Paperback 13-digit ISBN: 978-1-60754-048-9
6 pack 13-Digit ISBN: 978-1-60754-049-6

Manufactured in China

Credits:
Editor: Louise John
Designer: D.R. Ink
Photography: Gareth Boden
Production: Jenny Mulvanney

With thanks to our models:
Yim Poonsen, Rena Jutla, Louise John, Edward Higgins, Alex Evans, and Lewis
Robertson.

The Treasure Map

Everyone is making treasure maps. There is one piece of gold paper left.

4

"It's mine!"
says Rena.
"I want it!"
says Yim.

5

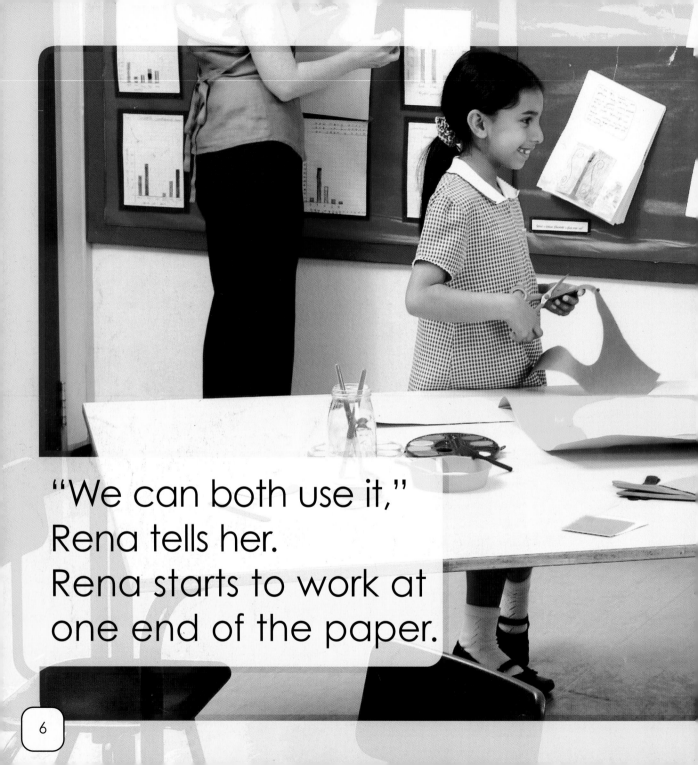

"We can both use it,"
Rena tells her.
Rena starts to work at
one end of the paper.

Yim agrees.
She works at
the other end.

They make the
treasure map
together.

"It looks great," thinks Yim.

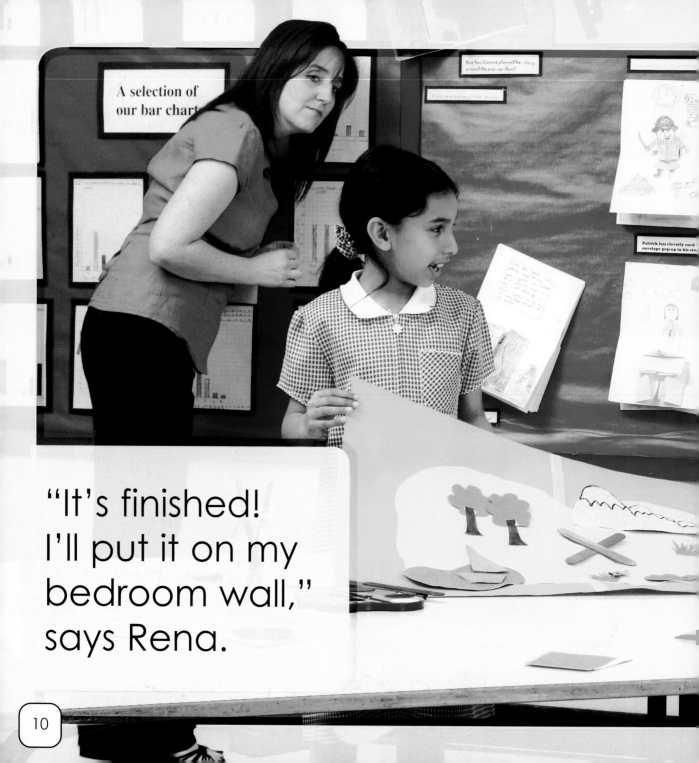

"It's finished! I'll put it on my bedroom wall," says Rena.

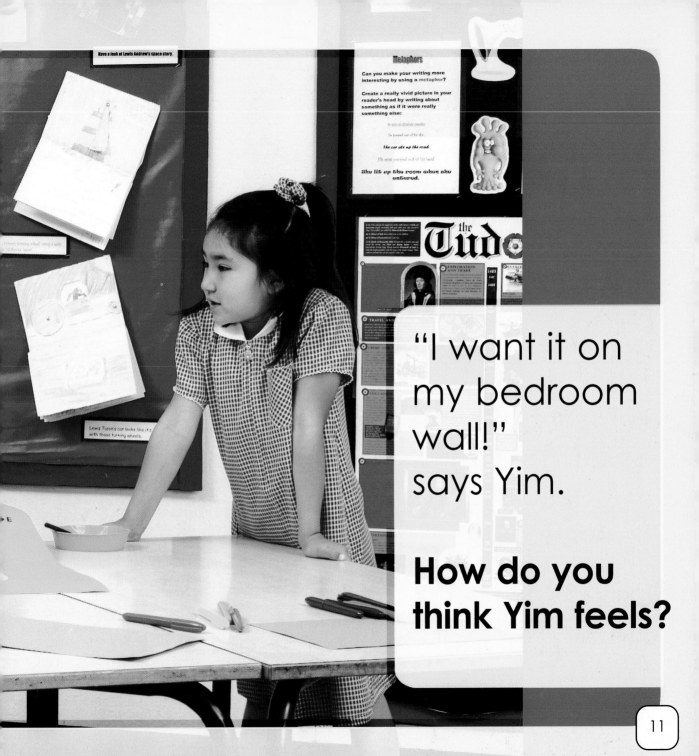

"I want it on my bedroom wall!" says Yim.

How do you think Yim feels?

"I've got an idea,"
Miss Johnson tells them.
"Would you like to hear it?"

"One of you could take it home today. The other can take it home tomorrow."

"Yes, let's take turns!" says Rena.

"Who'll go first?" wonders Yim.
"You can!" offers Rena.

When it's time to go home,
Yim rolls up the map
carefully.
"Thanks, Rena," she says.
"Tomorrow it's your turn!"

The Tiger Mask

Lewis comes to play at Edward's house.

Edward has a
new mask.
It is a tiger mask.

Edward puts it on
and growls.
"Grr!"

Edward paces around
the room like a tiger.
"Grr! Grr!"

"I want it!"
says Lewis.
He grabs the
mask.

Edward pulls away.
"It's mine!" he shouts.

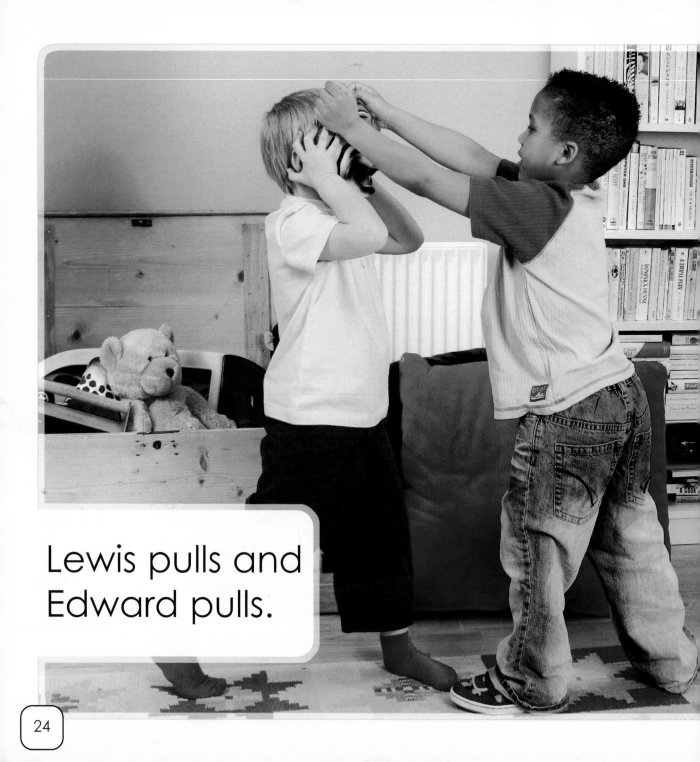

Lewis pulls and
Edward pulls.

The mask gets broken.

Edward starts
to cry.

Edward's mom comes over. "Oh, it's broken," she says. "What can we do?"

"We can fix it.
We can stick it
back together,"
says Lewis.

Edward gets
the tape.
Together they
fix the mask.

Now Edward is a tiger again.

And Lewis
has found a
giraffe mask
to play with.

FOR FURTHER READING

INFORMATION BOOKS

Carlson, Nancy. *How to Lose all Your Friends*. New York: Puffin, 1997.

Krasny Brown, Laurie. *How to Be a Friend: a Guide to Making Friends and Keeping Them*. Boston: Little, Brown Young Readers, 2001.

FICTION

Grindley, Sally. *The Big What Are Friends For? Storybook*. New York: Kingfisher, 2002.

AUTHOR BIO

Janine has worked in publishing as an editor and author, as a lecturer in education. Her interests are in personal growth and raising self-esteem and she works with educators, child psychologists and specialists in mediation. She has written more than fifty books for children. Many of her titles deal with first time experiences and emotional health issues such as Bullying, Death, and Divorce.

You can find more great fiction and nonfiction from Windmill Books at windmillbks.com